The PINK PAN[THER] in the Haunt[ed House]

by Kennon Graham

illustrated by Darrell Baker / Jason Studios

 GOLDEN PRESS
Western Publishing Company, Inc.
Racine, Wisconsin

The Pink Panther looked at the old house. "This is the tenth place you've shown me," he told the real estate salesman. "It's cheap enough, but it looks a bit run-down."

"Nonsense!" cried the salesman. "A different roof, a few walls, some flooring, and the place will look just like new!"

"When you explain it like that, I can see what a bargain it is," the Pink Panther agreed. "I'll take it! Here's your money."

"And here's your key!" the salesman said. "Congratulations! Now, if you'll excuse me, I must go!"

"What's your hurry?" the Pink Panther asked. "Can't you stay awhile?"

"Not a chance!" the salesman answered. "Er . . . that is . . . I have another appointment. See you around —I hope!"

"Hmmm," said the Pink Panther as the car disappeared. "Nervous little man. Acted as if he'd seen a ghost or something."

The house was dark. Dust and cobwebs covered the furniture.

"My, my," the Pink Panther said. "The last owner wasn't very tidy. Tomorrow I must clean this place!"

The Pink Panther opened the shutters. "That's odd," he said. "I feel as if someone is watching me! How silly!"

Now that the room was brighter, the Pink Panther spied a penny on the floor. "Aha!" he cried. "Find a penny, pick it up, and all day long, you'll have good luck! This *is* my lucky day!"

Then the Pink Panther yawned. "That reminds me," he said. "I'd better get some sleep. Tomorrow will be a busy day."

He made a pitcher of pink lemonade and found a book of ghost stories. "HAUNTED TALES TO SCREAM BY," he read. "Just the thing to help me relax after the day's excitement."

Whistling happily, the new owner started upstairs. "I keep imagining someone is watching me!" he said. "Ridiculous!"

Suddenly, from the attic, came a frightening noise. Oooooooo!

The Pink Panther paused to listen. "Gadzooks!" he said. "Sounds like an owl in the attic. Hope he doesn't keep me awake."

Just as the Pink Panther climbed into bed, there came another noise from the attic.

CLANK! CLINK-CLINK! CLANK-CLANK! JANGLE-JANGLE! CLINK-CLANK!

"Tsk, tsk." The Pink Panther frowned. "What a nasty noise! Must be mice. I'd better buy some traps."

He opened the book and began to read. " 'Once upon a time, in a musty, dusty house, there lived a ghost.

" 'One night a stranger slept in the house. The ghost slipped silently toward his bed. Slowly it came closer.

" ' "GOTCHA!" it screamed.' "

"Stop!" cried a voice behind the Pink Panther. "Stop that horrible story! I'll have nightmares!"

The Pink Panther looked around. "A ghost!" he exclaimed. "A *real* ghost! What a surprise!"

"Surprise?" shouted the ghost. "Aren't you scared? Aren't you frightened? Aren't you terrified? Anyone knows enough to be afraid of ghosts! Booo!"

"But I'm not just anyone. I'm a pink panther," the Pink Panther explained.

"You look like a pink pest to me!" the ghost snapped. "Anyway, this is my house. Shoo! Get!"

"Now, look here, Mr. Ghost," the Pink Panther
snapped back, "there's something you should know.
This is *my* house now. I just bought it. So, you see,
you're the one who must leave."

"Me?" gasped the ghost. "Leave? I've haunted this
place for years! Where else could I go? You can't do
this to me!"

"Dear me," the Pink Panther said. "That *is* a problem! Have some lemonade while we discuss this, panther-to-ghost."

The Pink Panther poured a tall glass of lemonade. But then he accidentally spilled it all over the ghost. "Oops!" he said. "Terribly clumsy of me!"

"You pink disaster!" the ghost cried. "Look at my sheet! I'm stained!"

"Tut-tut," the Pink Panther said. "I'll remove that spot before you can say boo!" The Pink Panther yanked off the ghost's sheet and skipped downstairs.

"Hey!" the ghost called. "This isn't supposed to happen! What are you doing? Wait!"

When the ghost reached the laundry room, the Pink Panther already had his sheet in the wash. "Be ready in a jiffy!" he called cheerfully.

"Well h-h-hurry!" the ghost chattered. "I'm so c-c-cold, I couldn't say b-b-boo if I wanted to!"

"There!" the Pink Panther beamed. "Good as new. Just as I promised."

He slipped the sheet over the ghost's eyes. It certainly was clean. But there was one problem. The sheet was no bigger than a handkerchief!

"Uh-oh!" the Pink Panther said. "The water was too hot. I hope you'll forgive this slight inconvenience. I think you should have been dry-cleaned."

"I've shrunk!" shrieked the ghost. He flitted about like a hummingbird with hiccups. "I'm ruined!" he moaned. "My haunting days are finished!"

"How true," the Pink Panther admitted. "But I have an idea! This house is big enough for both of us. Stay here and help me!"

The ghost stopped streaking about the room. "Help you? How? What good is a teeny-weeny ghost who looks like a dustcloth with eyes?"

"That's it!" the Pink Panther exclaimed. "You can be in charge of dusting!"

The ghost sniffed. He thought it over. He zipped down a dusty table to try out the idea.

It worked—very well!

"You know," he said, "that's kind of fun. I'd be pretty good at that sort of thing."

"Splendid!" cried the Pink Panther. "Then it's a deal!"

"It's a deal," the ghost said. "Except for one thing: I'll wash my own sheet. If you wash it again, I might disappear!"

"Panther's honor!" the Pink Panther promised. "After all, a good floating dustcloth is hard to find!"